First United States Edition 1990

*Margaret K. McElderry Books
Macmillan Publishing Company
866 Third Avenue
New York, NY 10022*

*Text copyright © 1986 by Catharine Gardam
Illustrations copyright © 1990 by Gavin Rowe
First published by Julia MacRae Books, London
Printed in Hong Kong by South China Printing Co. (1988) Ltd.*

10 9 8 7 6 5 4 3 2 1

Library of Congress Cataloging-in-Publication Data

*Gardam, Catharine.
The animals' Christmas.*

*Summary: One Christmas Eve a farm family discovers its
animals celebrating Christmas in a very special
way.
[1. Domestic animals—Fiction.   2. Christmas—Fiction]
I. Rowe, Gavin, ill.   II. Title.
PZ7.G162An   1990   [E]   90-5538
ISBN 0-689-50502-7*

The Animals' Christmas

Catharine Gardam

with pictures by
Gavin Rowe

Margaret K. McElderry Books
NEW YORK

High on a hill stood the ruins of an ancient church.
At the foot of the hill was a well-kept village
church. And halfway up the hill was Hawthorn
Farm, where Sam lived with his mom, his dad,
and his two sisters, Jane and Lucy.

It was Christmas Eve, and the children
gathered holly, ivy, and mistletoe.

Sam and his dad went into the wood
behind the farm and chopped down an
enormous Christmas tree. They carried it
down the hill to the village church below.
Two bushes on legs followed behind.

The church was full of
busy people, and soon
Dad and the children
were busy too.

When they had finished, Sam, Dad, Jane, and Lucy
set off up the hill. Far above them, Mom stood
at the farm gate. She was shouting and
waving in a most unusual way.
"I wonder what's up," said Dad.

"Oh! Oh!" cried Mom,
"the hens have gone, and
all the baby chickens!"

"What?" roared Dad.

"And Buster, the cockerel! I
can't find him anywhere."

"We must all hunt in the
fields," said Dad, and he
whistled for his sheep-
dogs to come and help.
No dogs appeared.

"Bess! Floss!" Dad yelled
in a fury. But the dogs were
nowhere to be found.

Sam looked into the cow
barn. It was empty.

"Dad! Dad! The cows have gone!"

"And the pigs," cried Lucy, peeping into the sty.

"And Binks," said Jane. "Binks, the bull, is not in his stall."

They ran around the farm, looking for the animals. Nellie and Harold, the two fat geese, were missing. So was Marigold, the turkey. All the sheep and both the rams were gone from the field. Even Jackson, the cat, and her three little kittens were not by the fire as usual.

"Call the police!"
bellowed Dad, and
he tore his hair.

Mom rushed to the
telephone.

By the time the policeman came panting
up the hill, it was snowing very hard. He
helped the family hunt through the fields again,
but it was getting darker and darker and
colder and colder, and there was no sign
of the animals.

Down the hill, through the dark night and swirling snow, the windows of the village church glowed with candlelight.
The bells began to ring, calling everyone to church to celebrate Christmas.

"Now then," said Mom, "we are all going to church."

"No, we are not!" shouted Dad. "We must keep looking for the animals."

"You are coming to church with the rest of us," said Mom in a quiet, determined voice.

"I'll come too," said the policeman, and he and Mom marched Dad and the children down through the thick snow to the little path that led to the church.

When they arrived, the service had already begun.
The candles shone brightly and everybody sang:
"Hark the herald angels sing,
   Glory to the newborn King. . . ."

Soon Dad was enjoying himself so much that he
stopped fretting about the animals, and sang and sang:
"Peace on earth, and mercy mild,
God and sinners reconciled. . . ."

Everyone came out of the church, then stopped still and stared up the hill. For the sky was filled with a soft golden light, coming down from the ruined church above. A curious sound drifted down on the breeze.

"Come on!" cried Sam. "Let's go and see." He raced off through the snow, with all the others following as fast as possible.

As they climbed nearer the ruins, the sound grew louder and louder. It was a strange sort of singing, and when Sam peeped through the old broken doorway he saw the strange singers. For there were all the animals, singing with the angels.

And soon everyone
shared in the animals'
Christmas.
"Hark, the herald
angels sing,
Glory to the
newborn King!"